Mr Parker looked towa
Billy Simpkins was st
the boy!

"*Billy!* I'm counting to five . . . "

Billy clutched his brushes in one hand, his pot of dirty water in the other and gripped his painting between the knuckles of both clenched fists –

" . . . One! . . . "

– Billy started running –

" . . . Two! . . . "

– the painting started to slip –

" . . . Three! . . . "

– and fell to the floor.

" . . . Four! . . . "

Billy's foot hit the slimy surface of the painting –

" . . . Look out! . . . "

– and the water pot shot out of his hand, and a tidal wave of filthy water swept across the pile of paintings on Mr Parker's desk!

BILLY
AND THE
MAN-EATING
PLANT

Mick Gowar

Illustrated by Denzil Walker

RED FOX

A Red Fox Book
Published by Random Century Children's Books
20 Vauxhall Bridge Road, London SW1V 2SA

A division of the Random Century Group
London Melbourne Sydney Auckland
Johannesburg and agencies throughout the world

First published by Macmillan Children's Books 1988

Red Fox edition 1991

Printed and bound in Great Britain by
Cox & Wyman Ltd, Reading, Berkshire

ISBN 0 09 981500 1

To Laurence

One

It was a cold, foggy afternoon in March. The village of Holebridge was wrapped in a damp grey haze. The fog had turned the police station, the three shops, the fire station and the church into grey plasticine blobs. Everywhere, the hard straight lines of walls, houses and fences smudged and blurred and began to disappear as the fog grew thicker.

At the far end of the village, the school glowed like a pigmy lighthouse. Every light in every room burned brightly, even though it was only two o'clock. In the four classrooms, children fidgeted and whispered as they waited for afternoon school to begin.

In Class Four, Mr Parker had nearly finished taking the afternoon register.

"Neelam Patel?"

"Here, sir!"

"Martin Quilley?"

"Here, sir!"

"Christine Robinson?"

"Here, sir!"

" – and finally, Billy Simpkins?"

No reply.

Mr Parker looked up. Billy Simpkins was sitting at a table on the far side of the room. His eyes gazed, glassy and unblinking, like a goldfish's. His mouth was half-open. Billy was a million miles away, daydreaming – again!

"*Billy!* Wake up and pay attention! I said: 'Billy Simpkins?' "

"Oh – here, sir! – Sorry, sir!"

Mr Parker bent over the register again. Very carefully, he drew a small black tick in the column next to Billy's name. It was a perfect tick – exactly the same size, and at the same slant as every other tick on the page. Mr Parker waited a second to make sure the ink was dry . . . then he closed the register.

In front of him, grouped around six tables, were twenty-eight children. Normally, they would be starting to wriggle and chatter and giggle by now. But today was special. Today was different. Today there wasn't a sound from anyone.

Mr Parker could feel the excitement of the class, but he wasn't going to hurry. No – first things first. He placed the register in the drawer of his table labelled "Register", and laid his black roller-ball pen in front of him so that it was exactly in line with the far edge of the table. Only then did he look up at his class of third- and fourth-year Juniors.

They were silent and tense, like sprinters waiting for the starting gun.

It was a very special day for Mr Parker's class. The children were going to paint pictures or make models for the "TV Young Artist of the Year Competition". Normally, Mr Parker didn't like the children doing things like painting, modelling and

2

glueing. It was too messy, and Mr Parker liked everything in his classroom to be neat and clean and tidy. But an important competition – that was different. Especially as it had been Mr Parker's idea for Holebridge School to enter!

Mr Parker cleared his throat, then stood up.

"Right, boys and girls – you all know what you're doing. Hands up those who are doing clay models – "

Half a dozen hands shot up.

" – you'll be working on the two corner tables. And please, try and keep the clay on the plastic sheets, not on the floor!"

He paused to let the message sink in.

"Painters?"

The remaining hands went up.

"Try to get the paint on the paper, and not all over the person sitting next to you."

Mr Parker looked round the classroom for trustworthy children.

"Neelam, Sonia and Matthew, give out the brushes ... Christine, Lucy and Thomas – the paints."

There was a sudden movement at the back of the room.

"Billy Simpkins!" snapped Mr Parker. "Sit down and stay where you are!"

"That's the last thing I need," thought Mr Parker, "Billy Simpkins crashing about, getting in everyone's way and knocking things over!"

Billy was the scruffiest boy in the class. He had

3

straight hair the colour of carrots, which hung in untidy flaps over his forehead and ears. No matter how carefully he dressed, the back of his shirt always escaped from his trousers and one shoelace always trailed behind him like a faithful pet worm.

Billy wasn't naughty, Mr Parker knew that, it was just that he got so keen and excited about things like competitions and projects. And when Billy got excited, he got clumsy. And when Billy got clumsy, anything might happen! That was what Mr Parker was afraid of. He didn't want any accidents – not today.

Mr Parker watched as his hand-picked helpers lined up at the art cupboard. No pushing, no shoving. They waited quietly and patiently for their turn to go into the narrow storeroom between the sinks and the coat pegs.

Mr Parker was very pleased. Even though it was an art lesson, his room was still neat and clean and tidy. He turned round and looked at the blackboard.

"Aaaaaah!"

Mr Parker couldn't stop himself giving a sigh of pride and pleasure at the sight of the blackboard. Now there *was* a work of art! The day and the date written in green chalk, as always. Then the main heading – *Rules of the Competition* – in yellow. Finally, the rules themselves with the most important words and phrases underlined in red:

Closing Date: <u>end of term.</u> But all paintings to be

finished by Tuesday, March 19th (Today).

Mr Fairbrother (Headmaster) to pick one painting or model per class.

Mr Fairbrother's decision is final.

Mr Parker was right to feel pleased with himself. The end of the spring term in any school is the most dull and boring time of the whole year. It's the only term when there's *nothing* to look forward to. There are no plays or concerts to rehearse for, no sports day to train for. The spring term is just one wet playtime after another.

But this year, because of Mr Parker's idea that they should enter the TV art competition, Holebridge School was buzzing with excitement.

Everyone had noticed the difference, even Mr Fairbrother, the headmaster. That morning he'd stopped Mr Parker in the corridor and said, "Well done, Mr Parker. This competition of yours is a great success. We'll have to do it again next year!"

And no one in the school was more excited about the competition than Billy Simpkins.

Billy had a special feeling about the competition. When Mr Parker had first told the class about it, Billy had felt a tingle, a special thrill run right through him. And he knew, he just *knew* he was going to win.

Billy was even more certain now. Billy's daydream in registration had been about the picture he was going to paint. Billy had *seen* it – as clearly as if it had already been finished. And it was brilliant!

It was a picture of a wild elephant charging out of a jungle. Although Billy had been interrupted, he could still see it when he closed his eyes: the great curving tusks; the ears spread wide like the sails of an old-fashioned sailing ship in a storm.

But Billy knew that he had to start painting soon. If he couldn't, the picture in his mind's eye would start fading away to nothing . . . like all his other pictures.

Billy stood up, and looked across the classroom to the art cupboard. Why hadn't he been given his brushes yet? What had happened to the paints? Billy had to start painting – now! What was going wrong?

Billy edged two steps . . . three steps to his left. He could see the cupboard door clearly now. Typical! The queue of helpers hadn't moved at all.

"Why does Mr Parker always pick the wet wimpy ones?" thought Billy. They were still lined up, waiting patiently. Billy imagined what was going on:

"After you – "

"No, after *you* – "

"My dear chap, I *insist*, after *you* – "

"No, *no* – I was here first – after *you* – "

And all the time, the bright colours of the jungle, the stark dramatic outline of the elephant were growing dull and beginning slowly to fade, fade away . . .

Mr Parker was still admiring his blackboard when he heard the crash from the art cupboard. It was followed by a scream. Then Christine, Lucy and Thomas stumbled into the room, their hair and faces coated with a thick crust of orange powder paint. They were followed by a fourth child who was bright orange from head to foot. He wiped his orange face with the back of his orange hand. It was Billy Simpkins.

"Sorry, sir – I was just helping them – and the big tin of orange fell off the top shelf and – "

"I can see!" snapped Mr Parker. "Go and get cleaned up, all of you. Then Billy, you get a dustpan and brush, and clear up the mess!"

Two

It was twenty-two minutes past three. The finished paintings were in a tidy pile on Mr Parker's table; the clay models were just being packed into the kiln. Everybody had finished and tidied their things away – everybody, that is, except Billy. He was still working away feverishly at the back of the room. Bright splodges of paint covered the floor around his desk, radiating outwards like the aurora borealis.

"*Billy!* This is the last time I'm going to tell you – it's time to stop working and clear away!"

Billy's hand, which had been painting furiously, became a frantic blur.

Mr Parker's patience was wearing very thin.

"*Billy!* If I have to tell you one more time, I won't accept your painting for the competition! Stop painting *immediately!*"

Billy stopped, and dived under the table to pick up his scattered brushes.

Mr Parker turned to Matthew Evans, who was standing next to him.

"Matthew – you've got one of those alarm watches, haven't you?"

Matthew nodded proudly. His watch could be set, by the press of a button, to warble the first four bars

9

of the "Hokey Cokey" at any time he selected. "Accurate to within 0 · 005 of a second", that's what the instructions said. "As worn by American Astronauts . . . Made in Taiwan."

"Could you set the alarm to ring in five minutes' time?" asked Mr Parker. "And tell me the *very second* it rings. We don't want any accidents with the clay models, do we?"

Mr Parker pointed to the kiln where the models were to be dried. Matthew nodded. Mr Parker could trust him. He set the alarm and stared – unblinking – at the pulsing numbers.

Mr Parker looked towards the back of the room. Billy Simpkins was *still* painting furiously. Drat the boy!

"*Billy!* I'm counting to five . . . "

Billy clutched his brushes in one hand, his pot of dirty water in the other and gripped his painting between the knuckles of both clenched fists –

" . . . One! . . . "

– Billy started running –

" . . . Two! . . . "

– the painting started to slip –

" . . . Three! . . . "

– and fell to the floor.

" . . . Four! . . . "

Billy's foot hit the slimy surface of the painting –

" . . . Look out! . . . "

– and the water pot shot out of his hand, and a tidal wave of filthy water swept across the pile of paintings on Mr Parker's desk!

10

For a split second, nobody moved, nobody breathed. Then all at once Christine Robinson screamed, Mr Parker bellowed, "Paper towels – *quick!*", and children ran from all corners of the room to Mr Parker's table. Only Matthew Evans heard the soft "Da-Da Di Dum-Dum-Dum/Da-Da Di Dum-Dum-Dum", like a tiny robot, humming to itself far, far away.

"Sir – ?"

" – Not now, Matthew. Go and get some paper towels!"

"But sir, I – "

"*Matthew*, do as you're told, boy – and be quick about it!"

Matthew didn't move. He couldn't move. What had Mr Parker said, just five minutes . . . no, five minutes and twenty-five seconds ago? Matthew could remember it clearly, *"Tell me the very second* . . . " If he ran off to get the paper towels, something *awful* was going to happen to the clay models. He knew that, because Mr Parker had told him so only five minutes . . . and thirty-five seconds ago.

Mr Parker looked up from his frantic mopping. What was wrong with the boy – couldn't he *see* what had happened? Was he deaf as well as stupid? Mr Parker yelled at the top of his voice:

"*MATTHEW!*"

Never, in all his ten years of almost perfect obedience, had any adult ever shouted at Matthew Evans like that! The poor boy fled from the room with a howl of terror.

11

It was a quarter of an hour before Matthew dared to come back. By then the water had been mopped up, and the paintings were hanging like sodden dish-cloths across the tops of the radiators. Matthew crept in, still sniffing.

The sight of Matthew, slinking red-eyed into the room, made Mr Parker feel guilty. He shouldn't have shouted like that at Matthew, he knew. Matthew was a good boy, a nice, tidy, clean boy. He beckoned Matthew over, and put a fatherly arm round Matthew's trembling shoulders.

"All right, Matthew? I'm . . . er, sorry I shouted."

Matthew had to blink back his tears again. Mr Parker didn't understand. He didn't understand *at all*. That wasn't why he was crying. It wasn't Mr Parker shouting and losing his temper, it was the *unfairness*.

"But . . . sir . . . " he hiccoughed, "it . . . you . . . it was . . . you . . . told me . . . you told me to . . . "

"Well, I may have been a bit rough," explained Mr Parker, patting Matthew's shoulder, "but it *was* an emergency. You do see that, don't you?"

"But . . . sir," Matthew gulped, "it was *you* . . . you told me to tell you . . . as soon as my alarm – "

"Oh, *NO!*" Mr Parker remembered what he'd told Matthew. And he remembered the instructions on the special modelling clay, "No more than five minutes at full heat to dry to a hard professional-looking finish."

Mr Parker ran to the kiln and wrenched open the door. All that was left of the models was a few blackened slivers and a large pile of grey dust.

Just at that moment, Mr Fairbrother, the headmaster, popped his head round the door.

"Hello, Mr Parker," he called across the room cheerfully. "How's it all going? Well . . . ?"

Three

Mr Parker and Mr Fairbrother sat side by side at Mr Parker's table. They were sifting through the wreckage of the art competition. Some of the paintings were still damp and soggy, others had dried and wrinkled like the dead leaves of some bizarrely coloured tropical plant. Not one had escaped the drenching.

Mr Parker was grumpy and cross. Mr Fairbrother was trying to look on the bright side.

"You know, I'm sure it's not as bad as you think, Mr Parker," said Mr Fairbrother, doing his best to sound cheerful. "I'm sure there must be something worth sending in to the TV company. Look – what about this one?" And he held up a slightly blurred and smudged picture of flying ponies playing leapfrog on a fluffy orange cloud.

The sight of the pink and blue ponies frolicking made Mr Parker feel even more fed up. It was exactly the sort of picture that Mr Parker hated – sweet and sickly like condensed milk.

"Or . . . "suggested Mr Fairbrother, "why don't we just forget about today's paintings. Your class could paint some more tomorrow and I'll judge those instead. And they could make some more clay models, too."

Mr Parker thought about that suggestion for a couple of minutes. Could he bear to have another art lesson? More mess and more spilt water? Could he stand having more paint and modelling clay smeared all over his nice clean floor? And what about the competition rules? Wouldn't another try mean breaking the rules?

Eventually, Mr Parker shook his head. "No," he said, "it wouldn't be fair to the other classes. We all agreed – all paintings and models in by today. I'm always telling the children that it doesn't matter whether you win or lose, it's how you play the game!"

"All right, Mr Parker," said Mr Fairbrother. "If that's what you think best ... Let's start clearing these pictures away."

Mr Fairbrother started to gather the pictures into one large pile. Then he saw one painting which must have slipped off the table. He stooped to pick it up. "Oh dear," muttered Mr Fairbrother to himself as he looked at the picture. What on earth was it supposed to be? The painting was a mass of smudged grey squirls, like angry rain clouds. In the centre of the picture was a large orange footprint.

Mr Fairbrother was puzzled. He scratched his head. He turned the painting upside down ... it looked even worse! He turned the paper over. On the back was written, "Wild Elephant by Billy Simpkins, Class Four."

Mr Fairbrother sighed and shook his head. He put Billy's painting on top of the pile. He looked at his watch.

"Well, Mr Parker, it's five o'clock. I'm going home. I've looked at so many paintings I'm beginning to get grey smudges in front of my eyes!"

Mr Parker still looked fed up and gloomy. "Cheer up, Mr Parker," said Mr Fairbrother. "I'll have another look at them in a day or two. There's still nearly a week to go before I have to send the best from each class to the TV company. I'm sure I can find one that's not *too* bad."

"Yes, I expect you're right," replied Mr Parker. "Good night Mr Fairbrother."

Mr Fairbrother's footsteps echoed away down the corridor. Mr Parker was alone in his classroom. He felt depressed. He felt he'd let down the children in his class. They had been so excited about the competition, and so disappointed when everything had gone wrong.

What would happen tomorrow? Mr Parker shuddered. He imagined Christine Robinson sulking because her painting had been ruined. He could see Matthew Evans flinching every time he raised his voice above a whisper. Oh dear. The end of term was going to be as bad as usual, after all.

With a heavy sigh, Mr Parker put on his coat, switched out the light and closed the door. Another day finished. Six more school days to go before the holidays.

Four

The next morning, Mr Parker waited anxiously in the classroom for the children to arrive.

He'd hardly slept at all. All night he'd been tossing and turning and worrying and feeling guilty. He was sure it was all his fault that the competition had gone wrong and all the paintings and models had been ruined. There was only one thing to do, he'd decided – apologise to the children.

On the way to school he'd practised what he was going to say. He ran through it one last time in his head as the children began to file in from the playground.

When all the children were sitting down, instead of taking the register as normal, Mr Parker stood up. He shuffled clumsily from foot to foot. He cleared his throat nervously.

"Boys and girls," he began, "before we do anything else, I just want to say a few words about yesterday's art competition. As you all know, at the end of the afternoon there was an . . . er – accident."

Several children turned round in their seats and stared at Billy Simpkins coldly.

"Now, boys and girls. We all know what the word accident means, don't we? It means something that . . . er, isn't really . . . well, isn't really anybody's

17

fault. It wasn't *meant*. That is, it wasn't deliberate, was it?"

Mr Parker stopped. He hadn't planned to say all that about accidents. He tried to remember what he had meant to say next. "Well, anyway," he continued, "because of the accident, some of the paintings were splashed. And the clay models were ... were – "

Mr Parker realised he was stuck again. Blast! He'd forgotten what he was going to say about the clay models.

As Mr Parker struggled to recall the rest of his speech, Martin Quilley put up his hand. Martin had been one of the clay modellers.

"Yes, Martin. What is it?" asked Mr Parker, grateful for the interruption.

"Why don't we do it again, sir? You know, make some more models and pictures today, sir?"

"I don't think we can do that, Martin," Mr Parker replied. "After all, the rules *are* the rules. The rule was that we had to finish all our paintings and models by yesterday. If we had another day, that wouldn't be fair to the other children in the school, would it?"

From all over the room children shouted protests:

"Oh, *sir* – "

"That's not fair on us, sir – "

"We won't tell anyone, sir – "

"Oh – *please*, sir – let us have another go – "

"Quiet! Everyone – quiet!" Mr Parker had to

shout. "Mr Fairbrother and I had a look at the pictures last night. And honestly, some of them were hardly damaged at all. We'll still be able to enter the competition – "

"Oh, but sir. It's not the same. It's not our *best* work is it, sir?" Martin Quilley pleaded. "And you did say it had to be our very best work – didn't you, sir? And what about the models, sir? What about the models?"

Mr Parker could see now that he'd made a bad decision. But he had told Mr Fairbrother. What could Mr Parker do? He was sure it was too late to change his mind now. He could think of only one way out.

"All right, Martin. I tell you what we'll do. We'll have our *own* competition, just for this class. And," he carried on desperately, "you can write, and paint and make models. And there'll be prizes ... and everything!"

"Yeah!"

"Brilliant, sir!"

"When can we start, sir?"

"What's the competition about, sir?"

The questions came spilling out, one after another. With growing panic, Mr Parker realised that he didn't know any of the answers. He'd got carried away. He'd just blurted out the idea of the competition without thinking about it. What was he going to do now?

"Boys and girls! Quiet, please! The competition, the new competition, I mean, will be ... er, I mean . . . it will – start tomorrow!" Mr Parker paused. The class was quiet again, waiting eagerly to hear more.

Mr Parker continued, more confidently, "I'll tell you all about it tomorrow. So, for the rest of today, you'd best forget all about it, because we've got lots of work to get through today if we're going to start the new competition tomorrow!" The buzz of excitement grew again. "Come on – calm down! Quiet! . . . That's better. Now, if everybody's ready I'll start the register."

Mr Parker was in a tight spot, and he knew it. He had twenty-four hours to devise a new competition, and he didn't have a single idea.

Five

Mr Parker believed the proverbs he taught the children in his class. When he said things like, "A rule's a rule, and you can't break it," he really meant it. Another of his favourite sayings was, "Never break a promise."

When he got home that evening he made himself a quick snack of beans on toast. He didn't have time to waste cooking a fancy meal, he had a lot of work to do. He'd promised the class they would have a competition – with prizes – and he would give them a competition. Even if it took him all night to think one up.

As soon as he'd finished washing up, Mr Parker took his notebook and pen out of his briefcase. Then he sat down at the table in the living room of his small flat to work out some ideas for the competition.

First, he made a sort of shopping list. He wrote down *Things I need*, and underneath:

    1 Topic for the competition
    2 Prizes

Then he waited for inspiration . . .
Half an hour later he still hadn't thought of any

ideas. He stood up, and walked out to the kitchen and made himself a cup of tea. Then he took his tea back into the living room and sat down again. He looked at his watch: seven thirty. Only fourteen and a half hours left.

He tried to concentrate. What kind of competition should it be? Did it *have* to be just painting and drawing and modelling? What if there was another ghastly accident? What about some sort of competition for neatness? Yes! That was a good idea. Mr Parker wrote down "neatness" and underlined it twice. But what kind of neatness competition?

Mr Parker put down his pen and tried to remember the last competition *he'd* entered. But the only one he could remember was last year's Christmas raffle to raise money to buy the school a minibus. That wasn't much help.

Then Mr Parker remembered that when he was at school there had been *lots* of competitions for neatness. Every term they'd had competitions for the tidiest desk, the English book with the fewest spelling mistakes, the best kept classroom. And they'd had prizes, too – house points!

When Mr Parker had been at school, every child in the school had been a member of one of four houses. He could still remember the names: Sunflower, Jubilee, Livingstone and St George. And every time a child did something good, like coming top in a spelling test or picking up a piece of litter in the playground without being told to, they were given a house point. House points were little

22

squares of cardboard. Every child in the school had a special house point tin in their desk (usually an old tobacco or Elastoplast tin) to keep them in. At the end of every term all the house points were counted up, and the house with the most was given a cup. Actually the cup never left the big glass case that stood in the entrance hall of the school next to the fish tank. But like most prizes, it was the thought that counted.

Mr Parker shook his head. It wouldn't work. He could just imagine what Class Four would think about a competition for the tidiest desk: "Dead boring." And Holebridge School didn't have houses and house points. That sort of thing was much too old-fashioned. Anyway, he couldn't imagine even Billy Simpkins getting excited at the thought of winning a handful of cardboard squares. No, the prize would have to be something really exciting, something the children would really want to win.

He looked at his watch again: eight thirty, and still no ideas for the competition or the prize. Mr Parker stood up and stretched. He was getting stiff sitting at his table staring at an empty notebook.

As he sat down again, a bright cardboard box caught his eye. It was a box of chocolates he'd bought to give Miss Moneypenny, the Infant teacher, on her birthday. (It wasn't Miss Moneypenny's birthday until the following Wednesday, but Mr Parker always liked to be ready for things like birthdays.)

Mr Parker stared at the box of chocolates. It was a

huge box. It was full of the most expensive, most delicious milk chocolates you could buy. What a prize that would make!

But then Mr Parker remembered Mrs Robinson, Christine's mother. Mrs Robinson owned the health food shop in the next village. Mrs Robinson always made *such* a fuss whenever there was white bread in the school sandwiches at lunchtime, or treacle pudding for sweet. What would Mrs Robinson say? *Chocolates?* He might as well give the class a bumper tin of rat poison, as far as Mrs Robinson was concerned.

Mr Parker was in despair. The only idea he'd had all night, spoiled by Mrs Robinson. He looked at his watch: nine o'clock. Oh ... blast Mrs Robinson! And he wrote down in his notebook:

Competition prize – Box of Chocolates!

He had a prize, but still no competition. But he knew the competition would have to be about something the children liked doing.

Mr Parker turned to a fresh page in his notebook and started to write a list of all the things he could think of that the children of Class Four liked doing.

1   Games – rounders, football, netball
2   Plays – especially ones with fights in
3   Collecting things – conkers, seashells, mini-beasts
4   Singing – loudly

He read through the list. It didn't look very promising, but it was all he'd got. He went through it crossing things out.

First, he crossed out games. He wanted a competition that would encourage neatness. There was nothing neat about games. In any case, the weather was much too bad for games.

Next he crossed out plays and singing. Class Four had spent all last term working on the Christmas play, and next term they would be doing lots of singing to get ready for the school's summer concert.

That only left "Collecting things".

Mr Parker chewed the end of his pen and thought hard. "Collecting things". That could be some kind of project. Yes! A project! A project would encourage neatness and hard work. He could even give a special prize for the one with the fewest spelling mistakes. But what could they do a project on?

Mr Parker thought and thought. He made another cup of tea. He walked up and down the room. He sat down again. He looked at his watch: ten thirty. He was getting tired. He decided to take a break. He'd watch TV for half an hour, and then have another try.

He turned on the set. *Another* snooker tournament. He switched channels, indoor bowls. He turned over again. It was a gardening programme. He leaned forward to turn off the TV, but just as he was about to press the button, he heard the presenter say:

"Spring is a *very* exciting time of year in the garden . . . "

Of course! Mr Parker nearly kicked himself. Why hadn't he thought of it before? It was obvious, a project about *spring*.

Instead of switching off, Mr Parker turned up the sound. Then he sat down at the table again, picked up his pen and notebook, and began to make careful notes on everything the man said.

Six

Next morning, when the children filed into the classroom, Mr Parker was sitting at his table. In front of him was the enormous box of chocolates.

"Oooooh, sir! Are they for me?"

"Is it your birthday, sir?"

"Save the orange creams for me, sir. They're my favourites!"

"Sit down everyone!" shouted Mr Parker above the noise. But he was pleased. The children loved the prize.

"I'll explain all about the chocolates as soon as I've taken the register. Is everyone here? – Good, I'll begin . . . Tracey Ashton? – "

No reply. The whole room was bubbling with the noise of excited children. No one was paying any attention to the register.

"Tracey! *Everyone!* Stop chattering, and let's get on."

But all through registration there was an excited twittering and whispering. In the back row, Keith Hall leaned across and nudged Billy Simpkins.

"I bet they're for Miss Moneypenny!" he whispered loudly. "He *fancies* her – "

"Billy! Keith! If I hear any more whispering or giggling, we'll have a SPELLING TEST instead!"

The children calmed down. Mr Parker finished calling the register. As he stood up to write the date on the board, the buzz of excitement returned.

"Thursday March 21st." And then he wrote a heading: "Class Four Competition."

Mr Parker stopped writing, and turned round to face the children. "As I promised, today we start our very own competition."

He paused dramatically, and held up the enormous box of chocolates.

"And this is going to be the first prize!"

Instant uproar!

"What's the competition, sir?"

"What have we got to draw, sir?"

"Are they milk or plain, sir?"

Billy Simpkins was so excited, he was half-way out of his seat with his hand up.

"Ooooooh, sir, I'll give the paints out – ."

"QUIET!"

Mr Parker was beginning to think that the chocolates weren't such a good idea after all. He opened the drawer in his table labelled "Register" as far as it would go, put the box of chocolates in, and shut the drawer with a bang.

Instant silence!

"If you're going to be silly . . . " Mr Parker let the threat hang in the air like a bad smell.

The children knew what they had to do. They snapped to attention – backs straight, arms crossed.

Mr Parker let his gaze sweep slowly round the room like a searchlight:

"That's better. I'll start again."

He pointed to the date on the board.

"Today is March 21st, and that's a very special day. It's the first day of spring!"

Mr Parker pointed towards the windows.

The children turned to look outside. The sky was as grey as a miser's washing-up water; sleet was falling.

"Spring is a very exciting time of year!" announced Mr Parker. "New life is beginning. Lambs are being born, crocuses and daffodils are coming up. There's frog-spawn in the ponds, and the birds are starting to build their nests."

The children looked out of the windows again. They could see that the sleet had stopped; fog was coming down.

"The competition will be for the best project on spring," continued Mr Parker. "And above all, I'll be looking for *neat work*. I'll be giving lots of extra marks for neatness. That means – " and he stared hard at Billy "– no smudges, no blots, *no mess*! Oh, yes, and I nearly forgot – "

Mr Parker fumbled in his bag, and lifted up an illustrated dictionary for all the children to see.

"I'll be giving this special prize to the project with the fewest spelling mistakes!"

"Oooooh – OOOOOOH! Sir, *sir*! – "

"Yes, what is it, Billy?"

"Can we start now, sir?"

"Just wait a minute, Billy," snapped Mr Parker. "I haven't finished. No, you won't be able to start yet because the project is going to be about your garden."

Billy's mouth fell open in amazement.

"You mean . . . everybody's going to do a project on *my* garden, sir?"

Mr Parker gave a long sigh.

"Just let me finish *explaining*, Billy! Everybody will do a project on their *own* garden. It will be called: 'My Garden in Spring'."

And Mr Parker wrote the title on the board (in yellow chalk, of course).

"And here's the sort of thing you can do," and as he spoke, Mr Parker began to write a list on the blackboard. "Make a list of all the plants – all the spring plants – in your garden. When you've done that, you can draw pictures of them. Or better still, collect some of the flowers and press them.

"Can anyone give me the names of some spring flowers? Yes, Christine?"

"We've got lots of flowers in *our* garden," replied Christine. "*We've* got daffodils and crocuses and snowdrops and primroses in *our* garden."

"Very good, Christine," beamed Mr Parker. And he wrote down the names of the flowers.

Christine Robinson looked over her shoulder at the class. She had a big "Nah-Nah Nee Nah-Nah" smirk on her face.

Keith Hall, the hard man of Class Four, had once had a plan to tie bricks to Christine's ponytail and push her in the village pond, where a twelve foot pike was said to lurk! But he hadn't. Someone had told Keith that there was a law against being cruel to pikes.

In just a few minutes, the blackboard was full of suggestions for things to look for. Not just flowers – sticky buds, hazel catkins, frog-spawn and Queen Of Spain butterflies.

Mr Parker was delighted.

He looked round the room. It was marvellous! All the children had taken out their rough notebooks, and were copying down the list from the blackboard, without being told to.

Well, all except Billy Simpkins.

"Typical!" thought Mr Parker. "He's daydreaming again."

But Billy wasn't having a daydream. He was reading through the list on the blackboard with a sinking feeling in his stomach. Things looked bad for Billy Simpkins.

As the list on the blackboard grew longer and longer – as more and more children told Mr Parker what was in their gardens – Billy became more and more worried. He read through the list again. His garden didn't have *any* of those things in it. Billy's dad grew vegetables, *only* vegetables, which he sold to the local shop. Every other sort of plant – weed or flower – was pulled out, dug under or sprayed to death.

Billy had waited and waited for someone to suggest cabbages, leeks, early potatoes or curly kale. No one did. It was obvious. Vegetables didn't count! What was he going to do?

Mr Parker looked at his watch. Five minutes to go before playtime.

"Any last questions?" he asked.

Margaret-June put up one of their hands. Mr Parker knew what they were going to ask.

Margaret-June wasn't really one person at all, they were two – Margaret *and* June. But they always walked around together holding hands. They always went everywhere and did everything together. On most days, even though they weren't twins, they dressed the same.

The rest of the class, and Mr Parker too, had given up trying to tell which was which. Margaret and June had become one person – Margaret-June.

"Can we work together?" asked Margaret-June, their two voices blending in perfect harmony.

"All right," agreed Mr Parker, in a tired voice. "If you *must*."

Margaret-June smiled happily, and began to tidy up their one set of notes.

Billy was still lost in a world of his own. He stared at the board in dismay. The bell rang for playtime, but for once Billy didn't hear it. This competition was going to be tough, very tough. He'd have to get his dad to help. If anyone could find a project in the Simpkins's garden it was his dad. Billy crossed his fingers. "Please, Dad. Please be in a good mood tonight . . . "

Seven

"Dad?" Billy called, as he let himself in at the front door.

No reply.

"Dad?"

Billy looked into the living room. There was no one in there.

"DAD!"

No reply from upstairs either.

Billy walked into the kitchen.

His older sister, Eileen, was in the kitchen, hunched over the work top. She was making herself one of her famous snacks. Eileen was fifteen, and went to the comprehensive school. Billy watched as Eileen sawed great hunks off a brown loaf. This wasn't catering, it was heavy engineering.

"Hey, Eileen, have you seen Dad anywhere?" Billy asked.

"Yeah, he's in the garden. But you'd better be quick, he'll be off to the fire station soon. His watch starts at five."

While she was speaking to Billy, Eileen added another two slabs of cheese, a slice of ham and a large pickled gherkin to her sandwich. As Billy's dad had once said, "Eileen's sandwiches are a health hazard. If one dropped on your foot it would break all your toes!"

Billy walked out of the back door, and down the side path into the garden. Billy's garden looked like the Trooping of the Colour performed by vegetables. There was a square lawn in the middle, as immaculate as a parade ground. Around the lawn, standing to attention, were the regiments of vegetables. There were potato plants, cabbages, sprouts, and curly kale in dead straight rows, each plant an exact measured distance from the next. And at the end of each row was a flag of plastic-covered card with the name of each variety and the date it had been planted printed on both sides.

Billy's dad was on the far side of the lawn. He was crouched over a strange machine which Billy had never seen before. The machine had two long handles, a short squat body, two wheels and curved stubby blades which were mounted on two metal discs. It looked like what you'd get if you crossed a food processor with a lawn mower. The peculiar machine was lying on its back with its wheels and blades in the air. It was dead.

Billy walked over to where his father was squatting.

"What's that, Dad?" he asked, staring at the short stubby blades.

"It's a rotovator. No, I take that back, it's *supposed* to be a rotovator. The blasted thing won't work!"

Billy's dad turned round and clattered about in the tool box beside him. He took out a spanner, and began undoing a large bolt on the underside.

"What does it do, Dad?" asked Billy.

"It's a sort of mini plough," replied his dad. "You know, a sort of digger. Here, son, hold this."

And he handed Billy the bolt.

"And for heaven's sake *don't* drop it."

"Did you buy it, Dad?" asked Billy.

"No," replied his dad bitterly. "If I'd bought it, I'd have taken it back to the shop and asked for my money back. No, I borrowed it from your Uncle Jim. Just look at the useless great thing! I was hoping to have half the lawn ploughed up by now, but – owwwwww!"

Billy's dad jumped up sucking his knuckles. The spanner had slipped.

"But why do you want to – ?"

"Not now Billy! Wretched spanner – " and he threw the spanner across the lawn. "Look what you made me do! If you hadn't been blathering away at me . . . Do something useful for a change, and find the mole wrench. Oooooooh!"

As his father flapped his grazed hand and swore quietly, Billy searched the tool box.

In less than a minute Billy's dad had calmed down. "Sorry, son. I shouldn't have snapped at you like that. But I've got to plough up this half of the lawn as soon as possible. Now pass me that mole wrench, will you?"

Billy passed the wrench. "But why, Dad?"

His dad looked puzzled, "Because I need it to undo this bolt, of course."

"No, Dad, I didn't mean that. Why do you want to plough up the lawn?"

"Well," replied his dad, slowly, "do you want a new bike?"

Billy nodded.

"And a nice holiday this summer?"

Billy nodded again.

"Well, that's why," his dad said. "We can't do all that on a fireman's pay, so I've got to sell more veg. Pity though," he added. "Your mum had planted bluebells in this half of the lawn. They'd have been up any day now."

Billy's heart leaped into his throat. Bluebells! Bluebells had been on the list on the board. Bluebells were real spring flowers, the only spring flowers in the garden. And any minute now, his father was going to dig the whole lot up! Billy's only chance of a winning project, and it was about to be ploughed up to make room for spuds, or spring onions or rotten old cabbages!

"No, Dad! You mustn't! Not yet!" Billy yelled. "You've got to leave it till the bluebells come up. I've got to – "

And as Billy waved his arms in protest, the bolt he'd been holding slipped out of his hand and flew into the cabbage patch.

Billy's dad didn't hit the roof, he hit the sky! As he left for work, his final words to Billy were, "Find that bolt, even if it takes you all *night*!" And it very nearly did.

There was an hour left before tea. Billy spent it on his hands and knees, sifting through the soil between the young cabbages and Brussels sprouts.

As soon as tea was over, Billy was back among the vegetables, searching for the bolt by torchlight. By eight o'clock, Eileen had finished her homework and came downstairs to watch TV. Their mum was alone in the living room, darning a pair of football socks.

"Where's Billy, Mum?" Eileen asked.

Mrs Simpkins nodded her head towards the window, "Still outside, looking for that bolt."

Eileen walked over to the window and pulled back the curtain. Peering out she could just see Billy, stumping around in the cabbage patch like a large, bad-tempered glow-worm.

"Oh, Mum!" said Eileen. "We can't leave him out there all night. He'll never find it, he can never find anything!" Their mother shrugged her shoulders, then sighed and shook her head.

"He's got to learn, sooner or later, to control himself," she said. "He gets too carried away, always flinging himself about like that – "

She looked up, but there was no one there. Eileen had left the room, grabbed her coat from the hall, and was already striding down the garden path to where Billy was searching.

"Never fear," she called cheerfully, "Hawkeye's here!" And she began to search in the potato plot next to the cabbages.

Five minutes later she called to Billy, "Bring the light over here, I think I saw something glint."

Billy mooched over. "Probably a stone," he

muttered. "I know it landed in the cabbages."

"What," asked his sister, "do bolts and balls have in common?"

"I dunno," mumbled Billy. This was no time for stupid jokes.

"They both bounce!" replied Eileen, and handed him the missing bolt.

"HEY! That's great! Thanks."

"Ssssh, stupid," hissed his sister. "Not so loud. You're the one who lost it so *you* had better be the one who found it. OK?"

Back in the warm living room, Billy toasted his toes in front of the fire and sipped a mug of hot cocoa. He knew everything would be all right now. Dad would forget all about the bolt in a day or two.

But then Billy remembered the project. He knew it would be a day or two before he could ask his dad for a big favour, like helping with the project. And a day or two was all the time Billy had got.

Eight

Friday afternoon was planning afternoon. As usual, Mr Parker wanted everyone to plan their projects: to work out exactly what they were going to draw, press or write about over the weekend. They could also go to the school library to look at any books that might help them.

"Don't forget," said Mr Parker, "your projects *must* be finished by Wednesday. That means you'll have to do lots of work this weekend."

Christine Robinson put up her hand.

"Yes, Christine?"

"On Saturday, I'm going to draw all the flowers in our garden," she announced. "And on Sunday, I'm going to draw the frog-spawn in our pond."

She glanced round the room quickly to check that the others were listening.

"*We've* got a pond in *our* garden, sir," Christine repeated, in case anyone hadn't heard the first time.

"Very good, Christine," said Mr Parker. "That's what I mean by planning, everybody. If you all think about what you're going to do, like Christine has, you'll all do well!"

Christine smiled proudly and flounced her ponytail.

Lots of other children had ideas too. Matthew Evans said he was going to write a poem all about spring. Martin Quilley was going to draw pictures of his mum and dad working in the garden. Neelam Patel had a rockery in her garden. Her dad had agreed to let her borrow his camera to take photographs of it. Everybody seemed to have good ideas, except Billy and Keith Hall. For once, the two noisiest boys in the class had nothing to say.

Billy was stuck because his garden was full of vegetables, but Keith was stuck because his garden was full of motorbikes. Not even whole motorbikes, just bits of old bikes that his three older brothers had thrown away. Like Billy, Keith had searched and searched in his garden for a flower, a bud, a green shoot. Nothing. The only spring in Keith's garden had fallen out of the cylinder of a Honda 125.

Mr Parker walked across the room to Billy and Keith's table. "Well, you two, what are you going to be doing? Billy?"

Silence.

"Keith?"

Silence.

"You'll have to decide today," Mr Parker carried on. "You've only got until next Wednesday to complete your projects."

Billy thought for a minute. "I think we'd better go and have a look in the library, sir. You know, see what books there are on spring . . . and stuff like that."

Mr Parker looked suspiciously at the two boys.

"All right," he agreed reluctantly. "But no messing about in there. A library is a place to *work*, understand? And I'll be coming in to check on you. And if I find you looking at books on football," and he stared hard at Billy, "or soldiers," and he stared hard at Keith, "you'll both be in a lot of trouble. Right then, off you go. But don't forget, *no* messing about!"

Billy and Keith picked up their pencil cases and rough notebooks and left the room.

"Do you reckon there'll be anything in the library?" asked Keith as they walked down the corridor.

"'Course there will," replied Billy. "There's books on all sorts of things – prehistoric monsters, trains, animals – it's not just stories. We're bound to find something."

As Billy had predicted, there were plenty of books on plants, animals, nature. They decided to start with plants. They looked along the plant shelf. *Conifers . . . Wild Plants of Britain . . . Garden Flowers . . . What to Look for in Autumn . . . What to Look for in Summer . . . What to Look for in Winter . . .* There were so many they didn't know where to begin.

"I know what we'll do," said Billy. "We'll look at the biggest plant book in the whole library. It's bound to have masses of stuff on spring."

They looked along the shelf. Lying on its side because it was too tall and heavy to stand on the narrow shelves, was probably the biggest plant book in the whole world. It was called *An Encyclopaedia of Subtropical Flora*.

"What's *Subtropical* mean?" asked Keith.

"I think it's the posh, you know, scientific word for spring," Billy guessed hopefully.

The two boys carried the enormous book to a table. It fell open at a chapter headed "Insect-eating Plants". On the facing page was a large coloured photograph of a Venus's fly-trap at the very moment of catching a fly. It looked as if two green, taloned hands had clapped together and caught the fly between interlocked green fingers.

"Cor!" exclaimed Keith. "It looks just like Audrey wossname – you know, from that Horror Shop movie. We got the video of that last week. It was great! There was this plant that ate people ... Here, do you think there are any plants that eat people in this book?"

Keith turned to the index at the back of the book to find out.

At that moment, Christine Robinson came swanking into the library. She stopped dead when she saw Billy. "Oooh look," she said sarcastically, "it's Billy Simpkins and he's reading a *book*!"

Billy didn't say anything. In a proper fight he could beat Christine easily. One good sharp pull on her ponytail and she was blubbing like a baby. But she had a clever, quick brain and an acid tongue. When it came to fighting with words, Christine always won.

"Well, I wouldn't bother if I were you – Billy Simpkins," she went on. "Because *you* won't win, 'cos you're just stupid and clumsy. All *you're* good at is spoiling things for other people!"

Christine was still furious that her painting of pink flying ponies playing on fluffy orange clouds had been ruined by Billy's accident.

Billy couldn't stop himself, "Shut up you fat snobby cow!"

"Ummmmmm!" shouted Christine, loud enough for everyone in the library to hear. "Ummmmmm – Billy Simpkins! I'm telling Mr Parker! You used *rude words*!"

And she flounced out of the library, delighted. She'd won again!

Nine

That evening Billy walked home from school very slowly. He was thinking hard about the competition. He knew he had to win.

It wasn't just winning the prize that mattered, although he wanted the chocolates. What really bothered him was the thought of Christine Robinson winning.

Billy remembered what she'd said in the library, "All *you're* good at is spoiling things for other people!"

"I'll show her!" muttered Billy to himself. "I'll show all of them. Mr Parker, too. I'll win, and I'll give everyone a chocolate – *except* Christine Robinson!"

Billy walked down the hill towards the centre of the village, past the Co-op, the Post Office/sweet shop/anything shop and the butcher's. He walked across the village green and past the pond, which reminded him again of Christine Robinson.

He turned up the winding lane that led past the church and up to his house. Slowly he began the long plod home.

If Billy hadn't been walking so slowly, and staring mournfully down at his feet, he would never have seen the daffodils. But there they were – daffodils! Hundreds and hundreds of daffodils sticking out through the broken railings that surrounded the churchyard.

Billy stopped. He stared at the daffodils. He'd never seen so many in his life. Wow! If only there were daffodils like these in his garden, all his problems would be over. If only . . . Billy stared at the daffodils even harder. Could he? No, no! Billy had been told over and over again, "*Never* pick the flowers in the churchyard."

He looked at the daffodils again. Now, what his mum and dad had said was, "Never pick the flowers *in* the churchyard." But anyone could see that these flowers weren't actually *in* the churchyard – they were more, sort of, hanging *out* of the churchyard. And that wasn't the same thing at all, was it? And anyway, he thought, there were hundreds of daffodils. Maybe millions of daffodils. He didn't want many, just a few to press like Mr Parker had suggested. Surely no one would miss just a *couple*.

Billy could see most of the way up and down the lane. There was no one about. He peered over the railings into the churchyard. No one there either. Billy bent down and started to pick daffodils as quickly as he could.

Five minutes later, Billy let himself in at the back door. He unzipped his anorak, and laid the flowers one by one on the wooden bench beside the kitchen table. Some of them were a bit squashed, but that didn't matter. He was going to press them anyway.

Billy walked over to the fridge. He opened the

door, took out a bottle of milk and poured himself a drink. Then he noticed the trail of muddy footprints which went from the back door to the fridge. He lifted up his feet, one by one, and looked at the bottoms of his shoes. Uh-oh! He'd been so excited that he'd forgotten to wipe his feet.

"I'll clean it up before Mum gets home," he thought.

Billy kicked the fridge door shut hard with his heel. The fridge gave a shudder. Inside, a plastic pot tipped over. Strawberry yoghurt began to drip-drip-drip from the fallen pot into a bowl of chicken curry standing on the shelf below.

Billy walked into the living room, followed by another trail of muddy footprints. Eileen was sitting in the middle of the floor, a cheese and pickle doorstep in her hand. She was watching TV.

"What's on?" asked Billy.

"Something new," replied his sister. "It's called 'Muscle Hulk: Saviour of the Universe'."

Billy walked over to where she was sitting and stood beside her.

"Any good?" he asked.

"No," replied Eileen, glued to the set. "Load of rubbish."

On the screen, Muscle Hulk – a gigantic Viking – was eating an enemy spaceship. Billy sat down to see what would happen next . . .

"Right, you two – wash your hands. It's nearly time for tea."

Billy sat up with a start. It was his mum's voice from the kitchen. She was back from her job at the Post Office.

"What's the time?" Billy shouted.

"Nearly six," his mum called back.

Billy and Eileen had watched all of "Muscle Hulk", then "Blue Peter", and then "Cartoon Time". Two hours had vanished!

Billy tore out to the kitchen and grabbed his anorak.

"Oh no you don't!" said his mother firmly. "Your tea'll get cold. It's too late to go out and play now."

"But I'm not going out to play, Mum," Billy explained. "I've got to draw plants and things in the garden. We've got this project to do and – "

"You should have done it when you came home," said his mum. "I'm always telling Eileen: 'Do your homework as soon as you get home.' And the same goes for you."

"But Mum – "

"No arguing! If it was that important you wouldn't have wasted all that time watching TV. Hang up your anorak and lay the table."

Billy shrugged, "I suppose I can do it tomorrow or Sunday."

"What exactly is this project about?" his mum asked.

"It's called: 'My Garden in Spring'," Billy replied as he opened the cutlery drawer. "And we've got to draw stuff like flowers, and sticky buds and newts that we've got in our gardens."

"Well, you won't be able to go in the garden this weekend, will you?" said his mum.

Billy's jaw dropped. Why couldn't he go into the garden, what was going to happen to the garden this weekend? Billy remembered the rotovator, and his father's plans to plough up the lawn. Was that the reason? What was his dad going to do that meant no one could go in the garden? Dig it up with a tractor? Or a bulldozer?

"Why not?" he asked, dreading what his mother might say.

"We won't be here," replied his mother. "We'll be at Granny and Grandad's. It's Granny's birthday, and we're going for the weekend. You hadn't forgotten had you, Billy?"

"Errr ... not exactly," replied Billy. He had.

Just then, his mum saw the flowers on the bench. Her voice went all gooey.

"*Oh*, Billy! How sweet! Buying Granny that lovely bunch of daffodils! She'll be so pleased, she loves flowers – especially spring flowers."

She kissed Billy on the cheek, and picked up the daffodils and carried them over to the sink. "I'd better put them in water or they'll wilt, all right Billy?"

"Errr, yeah, I s'pose so. Thanks, Mum."

Billy couldn't think of anything to say. How could he tell her, "Well, actually Mum, I nicked them out of the churchyard for my project ... "? Billy was stuck.

"Hurry up with the knives and forks, love," his mother said over her shoulder, as she arranged the daffodils in a vase.

Billy started laying the table. He'd have to work doubly hard next week. No daffodils, and no chance to do anything over the weekend.

Mum began serving. Billy saw it was curry and cheered up a bit. Curry was his favourite. He put a forkful in his mouth. Uggh! It didn't taste like their usual curries. It looked different, too – sort of pinkish. Billy tried another forkful. Funny, it definitely tasted sweet, like strawberry yoghurt.

"No," thought Billy. "Can't be. I must be imagining things."

Ten

Billy had a great time at Granny and Grandad's. Although it was Granny's birthday, most of the treats seemed to be for Billy and Eileen. On Saturday, there was birthday tea, with cakes and jelly and trifle. There was even half a box of crackers left over from Christmas. Billy got a pair of clock-work teeth in his cracker. They looked like ordinary false teeth, but when they were wound up they went gnash! – gnash! – gnash!

Then after tea, Billy and Eileen watched a video that Grandad had hired especially for them: *Muscle Hulk: the Movie*. In fact, Billy had such a good time that he completely forgot about the project until Sunday morning.

Billy wanted to see the Muscle Hulk video again. He particularly wanted to see the bit when Muscle Hulk smashed up an entire fleet of starcruisers with his battle axe. The trouble was, Billy didn't know how to work the video machine, and his mum and dad and granny had gone for a walk, and Eileen was still asleep in bed. Billy went off to find his grandad.

Grandad was working in the greenhouse. He was planting what looked like baby bushes in brown plastic tubs. Seeing the plants reminded Billy of his project.

"Of course!" he thought. "I'll ask Grandad to help. He knows all about plants. If he helps me, my project will be brilliant!"

"Hello, Billy," said his grandfather, a little surprised. "What are you doing here? Are you starting to take an interest in plants these days?"

"Well, yes, Grandad. Yes, I am," replied Billy. "And I was wondering if you could tell me a bit about plants and things, because ... " And Billy told his grandad all about the project and the prizes. He told him about his dad's garden, and how there were no spring plants to draw or press or write about, only vegetables.

Grandad listened hard. Then he said, "I think I know where you're going wrong, Billy. It's simple, really, you're blaming the garden. It's not the garden's fault. Your trouble is that you haven't looked hard enough, have you? Have you been out and really looked? Down on your hands and knees? To see what insects and plants there are in the garden?"

Billy thought about the other night, when he'd been down on his hands and knees looking for the bolt from the rotovator. That wasn't what Grandad meant. Billy shook his head.

"There you are! I thought you hadn't." His grandad smiled. "Look Billy, from what you've told me, this project is about what *is* in your garden. You've been thinking about what *isn't*. You've got to

53

look for what's there – insects, buds. You'll find it all if you look hard enough. And don't worry about what everyone else is doing. What's wrong with drawing vegetables? Haven't you ever heard of *spring* greens?" And Grandad chuckled.

Billy nodded, but he was disappointed. He'd been hoping that Grandad could do better than that.

Grandad smiled again. "Don't look so glum," he said. "It'll be fun, you'll be just like the old plant hunters. Searching the jungle for new plants – eh, Billy?"

Billy laughed. Grandad was obviously pulling his leg. Plant hunters? Load of rubbish! Big game hunters, yes. People on horseback chasing foxes, yes. But *plant* hunters – what a daft idea! People didn't hunt plants. Plants didn't run away and hide down holes or in the jungle. It was like the things Uncle Jim used to tease him with when he was a little kid. Things like, "Go and get me the tin of striped paint from the garage."

Grandad could tell what Billy was thinking. "I'm not kidding, Billy. There really were plant hunters. Still may be a few, I don't know. They were explorers. They travelled all over the world – into jungles, up mountains – anywhere there might be rare plants."

"Why did they do that, Grandad?" asked Billy. He still wasn't completely sure it wasn't a wind up. "I mean, just to get a plant you could grow in your garden if you wanted to?"

"But where do you think all our plants came from

in the first place? Look at these – " Grandad held up one of the plants he'd been potting when Billy had interrupted him. "They're rhododendrons. They originally came from the Himalayas, the highest mountains in the world. Imagine, Billy, discovering them growing wild, maybe on the lower slopes of Mount Everest itself. They might even have had to fight off wild yeti to get them!"

Billy nodded. He'd read about yeti. They were nine feet tall, Abominable Snowmen who lived in the Himalayas. It sounded really exciting! "But wasn't it dangerous – I mean, just for a *plant*?" he asked.

"Why do you think explorers go to places like that?" asked his grandfather. "To discover things. Some go to make maps of far-away places. Others go to catch animals. These men went to discover plants. And it *was* dangerous, very dangerous. I know that some people think that plants and flowers are sissy, but these men were as tough as commandos, as fit as first division footballers, and as clever and as cunning as spies. But they still needed a lot of luck. It was worth it, though, Billy, because if they *did* come back with a new plant it was worth a fortune!"

Billy stared at the plants in their plastic tubs. "These were worth a fortune?"

"Yes, Billy," his grandad replied. "A hundred or two hundred years ago a rich man might pay hundreds, even thousands, of pounds to have a plant in his garden that no one else had. If a plant hunter found a new plant it was like, well, like

finding an oil well or a gold mine! Just imagine, Billy, being the first man to bring a rhododendron back to England. You'd be a millionaire overnight! You could buy anything you wanted – *anything!*"

Billy could imagine it. He could! Keith was always telling him how he was going to join the army, like his big brother. Billy felt left out because he could never think of anything really exciting he was going to do when he was grown up. Now Billy knew, and it sounded much more exciting than just driving stupid tanks, and shooting boring guns, and water-skiing. Fighting yeti! Being a millionaire! It sounded brilliant!

They talked for hours. Well, Grandad talked and Billy listened – spellbound! Grandad told the most amazing stories: about the spy who smuggled mulberry seeds out of China hidden in a hollow walking stick; about all the explorers who had tried to take rubber plants out of Brazil and failed, and about the one brave man who succeeded.

Billy walked back to the house. He'd forgotten all about the video. He was dreaming about all the real-life adventures he'd have when he was a plant hunter. He'd tell Keith all about it on Monday morning. Maybe Keith would want to be a plant hunter too, instead of joining the boring old army.

Eleven

On Monday morning Billy got the shock of his life. All the other children in the class had done *masses* of work over the weekend.

It was easy for Grandad to say, "Don't worry about what everyone else is doing." Grandad didn't have to see how much everyone else had written. Grandad didn't have to face Mr Parker, either! Mr Parker, however, was walking from desk to desk beaming. He was delighted. He'd never in his wildest dreams expected the competition to be such a success.

He stopped at Christine Robinson's table. Christine had drawn pictures of crocuses, daffodils and a sparrow flying up to a tree with a bundle of tiny sticks clutched in its beak. And she'd brought in a jam jar full of frog-spawn to show the class.

"Excellent work, Christine," Mr Parker said. "Excellent!"

Christine glowed. Then she sneaked a look over her shoulder to make sure that the rest of the class had all heard. They had, good!

Opposite Christine sat Matthew Evans.

"What have you done, Matthew?" asked Mr Parker.

"I've done a poem, sir, all about my garden. And

most of it rhymes, sir. Would you like to read it?"

Mr Parker nodded enthusiastically.

Matthew handed Mr Parker the pages, one by one. 1, 2, 3, . . . 9! Nine pages of narrow-lined paper, covered on both sides with Matthew's tiny writing!

Mr Parker remembered to keep smiling. "Very good, Matthew. I'll . . . er, read it later. All right?"

Mr Parker moved on to the next table, where Keith Hall had just finished karate chopping his ruler into neat five centimetre pieces.

Mr Parker steeled himself for disappointment. Usually Keith didn't like work about nature. Keith thought birds and flowers and trees were sissy. In fact, Keith thought that most of the things he did at school were sissy. Mr Parker remembered the last project the class had done: "What I want to be when I Grow Up". Keith had written just one sentence: "I'm going to join the SAS and blow things up!"

But Mr Parker got a surprise, Keith had done something. It was a large drawing of a woodlouse, lying on its back with its legs in the air. It was very lifelike, except for two large bullet holes in its side. Out of the holes spurted two bright red fountains of blood.

"That's er . . . very good, Keith," said Mr Parker. "But do woodlice *really* bleed like that?" he asked.

"Yeah!" replied Keith. "They do when you shoot 'em with a Martian death ray!" Mr Parker's smile faded, and he walked quickly round the table to where Martin Quilley sat. Billy Simpkins was in a cold sweat. Mr Parker was now looking at Martin's work. Billy would be next! In a minute, maybe less, Mr Parker would be bending over Billy asking what he had done at the weekend. Billy had to think fast.

His hand shot up.

"Yes, Billy?"

"Please, sir. Can I go to the toilet?"

"Can't it wait, Billy?" asked Mr Parker, a bit annoyed.

"No, sir," said Billy. "It's desperate!"

"Oh, all right. If you must. But be quick!"

But Billy wasn't going to be quick. He walked as slowly as he could down the corridor, counting each footstep, until he was inside the boys' toilets.

Safe at last. He waited. Was it time to go back? Had Mr Parker finished with Billy's table yet? Billy counted up to two hundred very slowly. He tried to imagine how long it would take Mr Parker to look at two children's work and move on to the next table. Billy counted up to two hundred again, just to be sure.

As he walked back through the door, Billy thought he was safe. Mr Parker was standing in front of the blackboard talking to the class.

" ... well done, everybody. You've all worked very hard. I can see it's going to be extremely difficult to decide who wins the prizes! I'm really looking forward to seeing all the projects on Wednesday morning – that's the day after tomorrow. So don't forget – " and he tapped the words on the board, underlined in red, "Wednesday Morning."

Twelve

At half-past three Billy came running out of school and down the hill to the village. He sprinted past the shops, the green and the pond. He flew past the church, ignoring the protruding daffodils, and up the hill to his house. The slap-slap of his feet on the pavement seemed to echo Mr Parker's words: "*Wednesday morning . . . Wednesday morning . . . Wednesday morning . . .*"

He ran up the driveway, and along the path to the back door. But he didn't go through it into the kitchen. He didn't make himself a drink or watch TV. Billy ran straight past the back door and into the garden, where he crouched on the path to get his breath back.

He looked around him as he gulped in air. He remembered his grandad's advice, "Look. Just like the plant hunters. It's all there, if you look hard enough."

Billy stood up, ignoring the stitch in his side. He walked slowly across the lawn. The rotovator was still broken, and the lawn was untouched. Now where had his mother planted those bluebells? Surely there must be a shoot, or a bud by now? His dad had said, "Any day now . . . "

Billy crouched down on the lawn, and slowly

61

began to crawl forward peering into the grass for any sign of a spring shoot.

Half an hour later Billy was still searching, still scouring the lawn for anything that wasn't grass. There was nothing, nothing at all. Grandad had been wrong. Billy had examined every blade of grass, and there was nothing to draw or press or write about.

He sat down and gazed around him at the vegetable beds. What a useless garden. There were no flowers or birds or trees. There was no pond full of frog-spawn, like Christine Robinson's garden. There wasn't even a lousy woodlouse like the one Keith had found in his garden. There was nothing but leeks, and grass, and cabbages, and potatoes, and –

BONK!

Billy turned round. Behind him, in the middle of the lawn, was a brand-new, real leather football.

A face appeared at the top of the fence. It was Winston, who lived next door. Winston was a year younger than Billy. Billy thought he was a bit of a pain. The one good thing about Winston was that he was always getting great new toys and games – even when it *wasn't* his birthday or Christmas.

Billy picked up the ball.

He flipped it from hand to hand.

"This yours?" he asked innocently.

"Yeah," replied Winston.

"New?" asked Billy.

"Yeah," replied Winston. "Dad bought it for me on Saturday."

"Nice ... " said Billy, and he bounced the ball a couple of times on the soggy lawn. *"Very* nice ... "

He could see Winston was dying to get his ball back. Billy took his time.

"Give us it back, please," said Winston.

Billy acted as if he hadn't heard. He turned the ball over and over in his hands as if he was admiring the stitching or the quality of the leather. He was enjoying teasing Winston.

Winston tried once more, *"Please* give it back – " No reply. "You can play too, if you like," he added, unwillingly.

"Sorry ... did you say something?" asked Billy.

"I said, 'You can play too'," replied Winston, getting really worried that he'd *never* get his ball back.

Billy made a big show of thinking about the offer.

"OK," he agreed at last, as though he was doing Winston a big favour. "But only if I can be Manchester United ... "

"Billy! Teatime!" yelled his mum.

Billy ran out of Winston's garden, through the side gate and up the path to the back door punching the air. Manchester United had won, 56–24!

"We are the champions! We are the champions!" he sang, as he leaped through the back door.

"What's for tea, Mum? I'm starving!"

63

"Spaghetti and meatballs – don't touch! And wash those hands, they're filthy. You're covered in mud. What have you been doing, that project?"

Billy remembered!

"Oh, no! Look, Mum, I'll have tea later on. I won't be long – "

"NO!" said his mother. "In, wash and eat. How many times do I have to tell you? Do your homework as soon as you get home! In any case, it's almost dark now. You'll just have to do it tomorrow."

Thirteen

"Please, sir?"

"Yes, what is it this time, Billy?"

"Can I go to the toilet, please sir?"

"What *again*? This is the third time this afternoon, Billy. Are you feeling all right?"

"I dunno, sir. I've got this tummyache, sir. And I feel sort of – peculiar, sir."

Mr Parker interrupted him smartly, "Well, I think you'd better go straight to the office, Billy. See Mrs Wentworth. She'll look after you."

Mr Parker didn't like any sort of mess in his classroom, particularly not children being sick. And Billy did look very green around the gills.

Billy shot out of the room before Mr Parker could change his mind.

Mr Parker breathed a sigh of relief. "Just in time," he thought. And he bent over Keith Hall to see how Keith's project was going.

Keith had drawn another picture, of a dead worm with a dagger in its back. The worm was lying in a revoltingly realistic pool of blood.

"Do you like the *blood*, sir?" asked Keith, smacking his lips. "Good – innit? I did it with me mum's nail varnish."

Mr Parker didn't reply. Keith continued, " 'Cos I

wanted it to look just like real blood, sir. You know – all thick and slimy!"

It was Mr Parker's turn to feel sick.

Billy hadn't been lying about feeling peculiar – well, not really. When he'd seen how much work everybody else had done, he'd gone all hot and sweaty. And seeing Mr Parker getting closer and closer to his table had made his tummy ache – with fear!

He walked slowly down the corridor to the school secretary's office. He knocked at the door, softly. No reply. He tried the door handle. The door was locked. He knocked again, louder.

"Go away, I'm busy!" said a voice from inside the office.

"But Mr Parker sent me – " Billy called through the locked door.

There was the sound of a key turning in the lock, and then the face of Mrs Wentworth, the school secretary, peered out.

"The office is closed this afternoon, so Mr Parker will have to wait until tomorrow. Unless it's an emergency – is it an emergency?"

Billy shrugged his shoulders. "He sent me because I was feeling sick."

Mrs Wentworth sighed and inched open the door. "Well, I suppose you'd better come in and let me have a look at you."

Billy stepped into the office.

"Stand under the light, and stick your tongue

out," Mrs Wentworth commanded. "Hmmm ... "
she thought for a moment. "Is your mum likely to be
in?" she asked.

"Yes," replied Billy. "She doesn't work on Tuesdays
and Wednesdays."

"What's your phone number?" asked Mrs Wentworth picking up the telephone on her desk.

"1691," replied Billy.

Mrs Wentworth dialled the number, and waited
for an answer.

"Mrs Simpkins? Hello, this is Mrs Wentworth
from Holebridge School. Could you come and
collect Billy now? He's not feeling well. It *might* be
nothing to worry about, but with all this 'flu about,
you can't be too careful, can you? ... Good, I' ll see
you in about ten minutes. Goodbye, Mrs Simpkins,
and thank you." Mrs Wentworth put the phone
down.

She was very relieved. Like Billy, Mrs Wentworth
had told the truth, but not the *whole* truth. It was true
that some of the children had been away from
school with 'flu, but what was really worrying Mrs
Wentworth were the school registers. That was why
the door had been locked. Tomorrow was the last
day of term, and all the ticks in all the registers had
got to be added up by tomorrow afternoon. That
was what Mrs Wentworth had to do, or rather what
she would *try* to do. The trouble was Mrs Wentworth
couldn't add up. She was hopeless at maths. It was
going to take her all afternoon, all night, and all
tomorrow morning – and even then she was sure to

have the wrong answer! The last thing she wanted was to waste the afternoon running backwards and forwards with plastic buckets and beakers of water for sick children.

Ten minutes later, Mrs Simpkins arrived. She thanked Mrs Wentworth, then she and Billy left.

Alone at last, Mrs Wentworth locked the door again. She always did that before starting any number work. Once, one of the girls in Mr Parker's class – Mrs Wentworth couldn't remember her name, it was the nasty one with the ponytail – had come into the office when Mrs Wentworth was counting the dinner money. Later that day, Mrs Wentworth had overheard her in the corridor telling another child, "Do you know? Mrs Wentworth has to use her *fingers* to count the dinner money! Honest, I saw her – just like an *Infant!*" Since then, she had always locked the door before she did any adding up.

Half an hour later Mrs Wentworth was still counting the first register, "One hundred and sixteen . . . one hundred and seventeen . . . one hundred and – "

Ring-ring! . . . Ring-ring! . . . Ring-ring!

Mrs Wentworth picked up the phone, "Hello, this is – "

She was interrupted by a cheery male voice, "Right. Have you got a pen and paper handy?"

"Yes," replied Mrs Wentworth, still dazed from all the ticks and all the numbers.

"OK. Take this down: I'll have a number sixteen; a

number thirty-two – but without the prawns; a sixty-four with chilli sauce; and a double portion of fried rice. And I'll be round to pick it up in fifteen minutes."

"I *beg* your pardon," said Mrs Wentworth, in her iciest voice. "This is Holebridge School!"

"Oh . . . " said the voice. "You mean, you're *not* the Wang Poo Chinese Take-away?"

"NO!" replied Mrs Wentworth.

"Sorry," said the man. The line went dead.

Mrs Wentworth put down the phone, and turned back to the open register with a sinking feeling in the pit of her stomach. "Now, where was I?" she muttered to herself. "One hundred and twenty? No . . . a hundred and twelve? . . . " She'd forgotten! She went back to the top of the register: "One, two, three . . . "

Fourteen

Billy was sitting up in bed. He'd been home for an hour, and was now feeling fine. That is, he wasn't feeling sick any more, but he was still in a panic about his project, and his mum was refusing to let him get out of bed!

"But, Mum," he pleaded, "I've got to go out in the garden, I've *got* to!"

"Absolutely not," replied his mother. "You were sent home from school because you're supposed to be ill." His mum stared hard at Billy. She wasn't convinced by this mystery illness of his, not convinced at all. He'd recovered much too quickly, but if he thought he could be sent home and then spend all afternoon playing in the garden . . . well, he could just think again!

"But, Mum – "

"I said no, Billy," said his mother firmly. "If you're too ill for school, you're too ill to be larking about in the garden!"

But, Mum – "

"That's *enough*, Billy. I don't want to hear another word about it. You're not going out into the garden, and that's *final*!" And with that Mrs Simpkins walked out of Billy's room and shut the door firmly behind her.

Billy couldn't believe it! He'd escaped from Mr Parker and now he was in even worse trouble. What could he do? He'd never win the competition now, he'd never even *start*. He was stuck in his room, like a prisoner.

He tried to imagine what it would be like tomorrow, what Mr Parker would say to him when he found out that Billy had done nothing at all. And Christine Robinson. He couldn't bear to think of what she'd say. "Told you so . . . you're no good . . . nah-nah-nee-nah-nah." Billy wished he was *really* ill. If he was *really* ill, everybody would feel sorry for him, and they'd all be nice to him. If only he'd fallen over in the playground and broken his arm or something, everything would be all right.

Even Keith, his best mate, would take the mick. He'd told Keith all about how he was going to be the most famous plant hunter in the world. How he was going to climb mountains and canoe along the river Amazon. And fight wild animals and vicious cannibals. He'd told Keith he was going to win the competition, "Easy-peasy!" Now, Billy knew, he'd be lucky to even *enter* the competition. Win it? Not a hope!

Just then, Eileen burst into his room without knocking. "Have you seen my history book? I know it was somewhere in the house yesterday, and if I don't find it by tomorrow I'm dead – " She stopped suddenly. She'd seen Billy's face. It was longer than a snooker tournament.

"Hey, what's the matter with you? You look like you've lost a fiver and found a shirt button!"

71

Billy was on the verge of tears, "It's this rotten project. I wanted to win the competition and the chocolates, and now Christine Robinson will, and everyone's written pages, and Mr Parker'll kill me, and now I'll never climb mountains and fight yeti – "

But Eileen had her eyes shut tight, and her hands clamped over her ears. "Stop!" she pleaded. "I can't understand a single word you're saying. Now, take a deep breath. That's the way. And start from the beginning, *slowly* . . . "

So Billy told her about the competition and the prize. He told her about how he wanted to be a famous plant hunter, like the people Grandad had told him about. And he told her about how much work everybody else had done, and how he'd meant to work really hard but hadn't.

There was a long pause. Eileen was thinking. One minute. Two minutes. Billy could hardly bear the suspense!

Eventually she gave a big sigh. "I give up," she admitted. "The only thing I can think of is for you to play possum. You know, play dead. If you're off sick tomorrow, there *may* be a chance that old Parker will have forgotten all about it by the beginning of next term. One thing's for certain, though, you'll never catch up with the others."

"You mean, there's nothing I can do?" Billy could hardly believe that there was no hope at all. Eileen shook her head. "Nope. I think you've *really* fallen in it this time – head first! Mind you," she added, "if

you really were one of those planters – or whatever
they are – and you did find a new plant, that would
make their stupid drawings of boring old crocuses
look pretty useless. But it would have to be something really amazing – like a *triffid*, or something
like that."

Billy suddenly got excited. There was a way, after
all. Good old Eileen! "Where can I find a triffid?" he
asked eagerly.

Eileen laughed. "In a book! Sorry, it was just a
joke. Triffids don't exist, they're in this book I've
been reading in English. A triffid is a man-eating
plant that walks around and grabs people. Then it
swallows them – in one gulp! But it's just made up,
Billy. Like in a horror film. No one's ever really
seen one."

Eileen walked over to the door. "If you take my
tip, you'll be sick tomorrow. When Mum comes in to
wake you in the morning try and imagine something revolting – like drinking a mug of lukewarm
chip fat. You'll look so ill, she'll keep you in for a
week! It always works for me. Cheers!"

Billy was alone again. He tried to think about chip
fat . . . boils . . . cold slimy bacon fat . . . snot. No, it
wasn't going to work. Being best mates with Keith
Hall, Billy could imagine much nastier things than
that without feeling sick. If only there really *were*
such things as triffids.

Then Billy remembered the picture of the Venus's
fly-trap that he and Keith had looked at in the
library. He remembered the green hands with their

grasping fingers. What if he *made* a triffid? Nobody would know, would they? After all, Eileen *had* said that nobody had ever seen one. What if he did what they did on horror movies – took a plant and made it *into* a triffid. Yes! It could work. He probably had everything he needed to make a triffid right here! He walked across his bedroom to the cupboard and pulled out his old toy box. He emptied it on to the floor. Then he emptied all his drawers on to the floor. It was just a question of searching until he'd found everything he needed – just like Grandad had said.

Fifteen

It took Billy half an hour to find almost everything. He laid all the pieces out on his table. First there was the set of clockwork teeth from Granny's birthday cracker that went gnash! – gnash! – gnash! when they were wound up. Next, a roll of Sellotape and a pot of green poster paint. Then last, and best of all, a pair of old rubber gloves with fur stuck to the backs. Mum had made them when he'd been a werewolf in the Cub Scouts' Christmas play. All that was missing was the body, and Billy knew where to get that.

He ran out of his room, down the stairs and into the living room.

"Mum, you know that project – "

"Huh? What? Who?" His mother had been dozing in the armchair.

"You know, the one about plants and things – "

"Eh? Oh, yes." His mum sat up. "Haven't you finished it? I thought it had to be in tomorrow."

"Yeah," said Billy. "All finished, except for something to take in. We're supposed to take in something to show, like Christine Robinson's got a pond in her garden and she's taking in frog-spawn. So I was wondering, could I take in the uggh plant, *please?*"

His mother turned round to see where Billy was

pointing. "Oh! You mean the yucca plant. I can't imagine why anyone would be interested in that ghastly thing. Well, I'm not sure, Billy. You're so clumsy – "

She looked up at Billy. He was pleading with his eyes. "Oh, all right then. But be careful with it. I can't stand the thing, but it was a present from your Auntie Babs, and you know how she fusses over it whenever she comes to stay."

She looked at Billy as he picked up the plant. "I almost forgot – how are you feeling? Are you sure you'll be up to going to school in the morning?"

"Oh yeah," replied Billy, "I'm all right now, it was just something I ate. School dinners are really revolting. Today's was like drinking lukewarm chip fat!"

"Uggggh! Don't!" His mother shuddered. "Anyway, even if it was that school dinner, I think you'd better go to bed early."

To her surprise, Billy agreed at once. "OK, Mum. I'll just take this upstairs, and then I'll go straight to bed. Good night."

Billy worked secretly, by torchlight, until after midnight. He'd never worked so hard in his life, and he hadn't really made much mess. He shone the torch round the room to check: only a little bit of green paint on his pillow . . . and on the sheets . . . and on the wallpaper. Still, he could easily clean it all up in the morning. And there, on the table, silhouetted in the torchlight, was Billy's project – finished! He'd done it!

The only problem left was how to get it out of the house tomorrow morning. He couldn't just stick something that size up his jumper. He gazed at the triffid. It looked great! It had green clutching hands, and at the top, the crowning glory – a vicious set of green teeth!

Billy turned the key behind the teeth: gnash! – gnash! – gnash! – gnash! went the teeth. In the half-light of the torch it looked threatening, horrible – and *real*! It was a winner, definitely a winner!

Sixteen

"Billy!"

Billy woke up with a start. It was his mum yelling up the stairs.

"BILLY! I'm not going to call you again! It's half-past eight!"

Billy leaped out of bed and ran to the top of the stairs. He leaned over the banisters and saw his mum standing in the hall with her hat and coat on.

"Hurry up, or you're going to be late! Your breakfast's on the table. Dad's giving me a lift into town, so you'll have to get yourself ready. And don't forget, take care of that yucca plant."

Billy ran back to his room. What luck! He'd been worried about how he was going to get the triffid out of the house without anybody seeing.

He washed, dressed, and carried the plant gingerly downstairs. Slowly, slowly, one . . . step . . . at . . . a . . . time . . . Even so, as he carried it through the hall to the kitchen, one of the hands started to slither down the body. By the time he'd got it on to the kitchen table the hand was hanging by one strand of green Sellotape. There was nothing for it, he was going to have to stick every piece down again or the whole thing would fall apart before he was half-way down the road.

79

Billy ran upstairs to get the Sellotape and paint.

By the time he'd finished it was twenty past nine! The fresh coat of paint was still very sticky. He'd have to wrap the plant in something. He looked around the kitchen. Yes! The tea towel, that would do nicely.

Billy draped the tea towel over the triffid, and shuffled to the front door with his precious bundle. It was going to take *hours* to get to school walking as slowly as this.

There were only five minutes left before playtime. Mr Parker was standing in front of the class, about to announce the winner of the project competition: "As I told you, every project was so good that it was very hard to pick a winner. But in the end I decided that the best project was – "

He was interrupted by the door crashing open. Billy staggered into the room carrying a tall lumpy object covered in a tea towel.

"Where *have* you been, Billy?" asked Mr Parker. "And what on earth have you got there?"

"It's my project, sir, " replied Billy.

"Your *project*?" Mr Parker stared at the strange lump. Then he looked at the pile of neatly labelled folders on his desk that all the other children had given in.

"Yes, sir," replied Billy. "It's a plant, sir. A *new* plant, sir, and *I* discovered it, sir. My grandad told me all about plant hunters, so I went out and hunted, on the Common, sir. And I found this plant that nobody's ever seen before. And I'm going to call it – "

Billy pulled off the tea towel with a flourish.

"A *triffid!*"

Twenty-eight mouths fell open as the children and Mr Parker gawped in disbelief at Billy's triffid. It was a vicious looking plant with a thick, stubby stem. Two hairy green hands stuck out from each side. At the top of the plant, where the leaves were tiny, was a gleaming set of green teeth!

Billy mistook the shocked silence for admiration. He continued with the speech he'd worked out on the long, slow walk to school.

"It's a bit like a Venus's fly-trap," he explained, pointing at the hairy green hands, "except it doesn't eat flies, it eats people – look!" And he turned the clockwork key. Gnash! – gnash! – gnash! went the green teeth.

"Can I open the chocolates now, sir?" asked Billy, as the playtime bell broke the silence.

Seventeen

As Mr Parker flung open the staff room door, all the other teachers leaped to their feet and started singing: "Happy birthday to you! Happy birthday to you! Happy birthday Miss Moneypenny ... "

The singing faltered and died away. Instead of a blushing Miss Moneypenny, a furious, scarlet-faced Mr Parker stood in the doorway.

Mr Parker exploded, "*Look* at this!" He held out Billy's triffid. "Just *look* at what he's done. I ... I ... I'll ... You'd better deal with him, Mr Fairbrother. I wouldn't trust myself! Just keep him out of my sight or I'll ... I'll ... *throttle* the little monster!" And with that, Mr Parker plonked the triffid in Mr Fairbrother's arms and stormed out, nearly flattening Miss Moneypenny, who slipped into the staff room unnoticed.

Mr Fairbrother looked out into the corridor. Pressed against the wall, as if by Mr Parker's slipstream, was a very miserable Billy Simpkins.

"Is this something to do with you, Billy?" he asked, holding the plant out at arm's length. Without looking up, Billy nodded.

"Well," said Mr Fairbrother, slowly and calmly. "I think we'd better go to my room and talk this over – don't you?" Billy nodded. He was still staring at his feet.

"Right then," said Mr Fairbrother firmly. "Follow me."

And they set off down the corridor, Mr Fairbrother carrying the plant, Billy trailing a few steps behind.

Half an hour later, Billy Simpkins left Mr Fairbrother's room carrying a written apology for Mr Parker. Head still bowed, Billy began the long, long walk back to the classroom.

Mr Fairbrother still wasn't sure if he'd really found out why Billy had been so desperate to win the project competition. Something about a box of chocolates and wanting to canoe up the Amazon and fight yeti. What on earth was Mr Parker teaching his class in geography lessons? It was the first time Mr Fairbrother had heard of South American yeti on Mount Everest!

"Blasted competitions!" Mr Fairbrother muttered to himself. "They're nothing but trouble!" And he gazed at the mess of paintings spread over his desk. Today was the day he had to choose the best pictures to send in to the "TV Young Artist of the Year Competition".

With a weary sigh he tidied the piles of pictures from Miss Moneypenny's Infant Class. They must have spent weeks doing them: twenty finger paintings, twenty potato prints, and twenty pictures of "My Family", grotesque figures with tiny bodies, huge heads, and leering mouths crammed with sharp pointed teeth.

In the end he picked Tracey Carter's picture of her family. It was the only picture where Mummy and Daddy's smiles didn't make them look like hungry sharks.

That left the Juniors. Oh dear! And Mr Parker's class. That was going to be the most difficult. What should Mr Fairbrother do? Leave it till after lunch, or get it out of the way? Mr Fairbrother decided to get it out of the way. The thought of those masses of grey squirls waiting for him would give him the most awful indigestion.

He cleared away the Infants' paintings, and picked up the pile from Mr Parker's class and spread them across his desk. Ugggh! They were even worse than he remembered. But he'd promised the children – one painting from every class. But what the children didn't know was that Mr Fairbrother had to write a report on each painting he picked, saying why he thought it was so good. Even if he could find one that wasn't *too* bad, whatever was he going to say about it?

Mr Fairbrother stared at the pictures spread out in front of him. All the smudges and blots made them look like the most crazy modern paintings. What were they called? . . . Oh, yes, "Action paintings". The sort of paintings where the artist threw paint at the canvas and then rode a bicycle over it.

Somewhere in his bookcase, Mr Fairbrother remembered, was a book on that sort of thing. He walked across the room and looked along the shelves: *Hymns Ancient and Modern . . . Stories for*

Seven-year Olds . . . Advanced Spelling Tests for Juniors . . . Ah! There it was – *How to Understand Modern Art*.

Mr Fairbrother went back to his desk and opened the book at random: " . . . one of the masterpieces of modern sculpture", he read. "A work of genius . . . "

Mr Fairbrother looked at the illustration on the opposite page. It was called "The Gift". The coloured photograph showed an old-fashioned flat iron, the kind that Mr Fairbrother's granny had used, which had to be heated over a fire. Glued to the bottom of the iron were rows of wicked looking nails. Mr Fairbrother was flabbergasted. It didn't look like a "work of genius". It just looked like a rather vile practical joke. "What kind of a gift is *that*," he thought. "I'd rather have Billy Simpkins's man-eating plant!"

Slowly, not quite believing the idea that was beginning to form in his mind, Mr Fairbrother looked up from his book. He stared at the triffid. It was squatting in the corner of the room.

Mr Fairbrother walked over to take a closer look. He hadn't really paid much attention to it before. He examined the body, the hands, the teeth. It was clever, *very* clever! If that ghastly iron was "a work of genius" what would some twit of an art expert make of Billy's plant?

"All it's lacking," thought Mr Fairbrother, "is a title. Now, what could it be called?"

Eighteen

It was THE BIG DAY! It was ten past five.

Billy's dad, his sister Eileen, Granny, Grandad, Uncle Jim, and Auntie Babs were all sitting in the living room of Billy's house staring at the TV set, hardly daring to breathe, they were so excited.

Grandad had plugged his video into the TV set to record every second! All afternoon he'd been fiddling with leads, and checking and rechecking to make sure everything was working.

The show started. Everybody was on the edge of their seats with excitement as the presenter said: "Later, we'll be meeting the winners of the 'TV Young Artist of the Year Competition'. But first, over to Sue . . . "

Oh no! How disappointing. First there was a long filmed report about what it was like to go to school in China. Then, just as the family was getting excited again, the woman presenter who always made a mess of everything, tried to demonstrate how to make a periscope using the middles of toilet rolls and bits of kitchen foil.

Billy's dad impatiently checked his watch again. Then the studio lights dimmed, and the jaunty male presenter put on his "serious" face. "And now," he announced solemnly, "the results of our nationwide

86

competition to find the 'TV Young Artist of the Year'. In reverse order: fifth prize for the under-sevens goes to . . . "

There was another groan of disappointment from the Simpkins family. They had to sit through fourth prize . . . third prize . . . second prize . . . "Come on, come on," moaned Billy's dad. "Nobody's interested in all *this* – get on with it!"

Suddenly Eileen let out a piercing shriek, "Look everybody! *Look* – it's BILLY!" And there he was, staring nervously at his feet, while the presenter said, "And now . . . the moment you've all been waiting for! The overall winner – our TV Young Artist of the Year . . . Billy *Simpkins!*"

Billy's family leaped to their feet clapping and cheering and jumping up and down! They were interrupted by Granny. "Sssh!" she said. "He hasn't finished yet."

"And now," continued the presenter, "let's have a look at Billy's winning entry – a sculpture entitled, 'Desperation'!"

And there was the short stubby plant with hairy green hands and gleaming green teeth. As the camera zoomed in to a close up, a hand could be seen turning a key which was half hidden among the tiny leaves at the top. Gnash! – gnash! – gnash! went the green teeth.

All the Simpkins family cheered again – well, all except Auntie Babs, who was staring at the screen with a look of astonishment on her face.

Billy walked forward and shook hands with the three judges, who hadn't said a word. The presenter

steered Billy round to face the camera.

"Well done, Billy!" he said warmly. "Now, as you know, the first prize is a cheque for £500 for your school to buy art materials. And here is a cheque for £150 for *you*! Tell me, Billy – and I'm sure everybody watching at home will want to know, too – what are you going to spend your prize money on?"

Billy hesitated. He knew what to say, but suddenly his mouth was dry and his stomach felt as if it had been tied in knots.

"Don't be shy, Billy. Is it going to be things for sculpture? Wood? Or chisels?"

Billy cleared his throat, and his voice came back. "No," he replied, "nothing like that. Last night – staying in that posh hotel – I talked it over with my mum. And I decided I was going to buy presents for everyone that's helped me with my . . . er, sculpture. My grandad, my sister Eileen, and Mr Fairbrother and Mr Parker at my school. Then, if there's any money left over, I'm going to go out and buy the biggest box of chocolates I can find, and I'm going to give one to everybody in my class – " Billy paused. "Even Christine Robinson!"